20 Ag 90

$12.88

DATE			

ST. CHARLES PUBLIC LIBRARY DISTRICT
ONE SOUTH SIXTH AVENUE
ST. CHARLES, ILLINOIS   60174

© THE BAKER & TAYLOR CO.

National Worm Day

by James Stevenson

Greenwillow Books, New York

Watercolor paints and a black pen were used for
the full-color art. The text type is Slimbach.

Library of Congress Cataloging-in-Publication Data

Stevenson, James (date)
National Worm Day / James Stevenson.
p.   cm.
Summary: Three humorous episodes in the lives of a
worm, snail, rhinoceros, and their animal associates.
ISBN 0-688-08771-X.
ISBN 0-688-08772-8 (lib. bdg.)
[1. Animals — Fiction.   2. Humorous stories.]
I. Title.   PZ7.S84748Nat 1990
[E] — dc19   88-34915   CIP   AC

« *1* »

NATIONAL
WORM DAY

"What's your hurry, Herbie?" asked Amelia.
 "It's National Worm Day," said Herbie. "Got
  to rush."
 "What happens on National Worm Day?"
  asked Amelia.
 "We elect a president," said Herbie, "and we
  sing the worm national anthem."

Herbie vanished into the earth.

"Where's Herbie?" asked Dawn.

"Below," said Amelia. "It's National Worm Day."

"I hear singing," said Dawn.

"Does it sound like worms?" asked Amelia.

"I think so," said Dawn.

"What are they singing?" asked Amelia.

"Shhh," said Dawn. "I'm trying to hear."

Amelia waited.

"I think I've got it," said Dawn. "Deep in our earth
so wondrous," she sang, " with dirt above us
and under us —"
"That's lovely," said Amelia.

Herbie came up. "Did you hear our national
anthem?" he asked.
"It was very moving," said Dawn.
"What's next, Herbie?" asked Amelia.
"The worm parade," said Herbie. "Got to go!"
"Oh, I love a parade!" said Dawn.
"Me, too!" said Amelia.

"Well, come on down and watch!" said Herbie.

Dawn and Herbie went below.

Amelia was left alone.

Amelia waited and waited.

At last she started home.

"Forward—march!" she said.

"Da-dum, da-dum, da dum-dum-dum..."

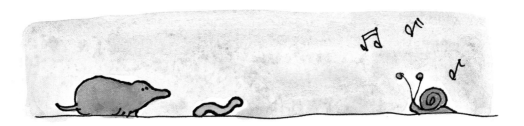

When Amelia got home, she began to sing,

"Hail to thee, oh mighty snail,

Oh mighty snail, to thee we hail."

Along came Herbie and Dawn.

"What's that beautiful song?" asked Herbie.

"It's the snail national anthem," said Amelia.

"I didn't know you had one," said Dawn.

"We do now," said Amelia.

«2»

RUPERT

Rupert was sitting alone by the water, thinking how nice it would be to have some friends. Just then a fish jumped up.

"Wow!" said the fish.

Then the fish flopped back into the water.

A few minutes later a frog hopped up.

"How about that!" he said.

Then he hopped away.

Soon a turtle crawled out of the water.

He looked at Rupert.

"They're absolutely right," said the turtle.

"Who's right?" asked Rupert.

"The fish and the frog," said the turtle.

"What did they say?" asked Rupert.

"They said if I came over here, I'd see somebody really big and ugly," said the turtle.

"They did?" said Rupert.

"Nothing personal," said the turtle, and he crawled away.

Rupert looked at his reflection in the water.
"I guess they have a point," he said. "I better
get used to being alone."
He walked away from the water.

Just then a beetle ran up to Rupert.

"Hey, pal," he said, "I need help!"

"You do?" said Rupert.

"I'm looking for somebody big and brave," said
the beetle. "Preferably with two horns."

"I have two horns," said Rupert.

"Why, so you do," said the beetle. "I need
someone who can bellow and scare people,
and who squashes whatever he sits on."

"I bellow a little," said Rupert. "And sometimes
I squash things by mistake."

"What's your name?" asked the beetle.

"Rupert," said Rupert.

"Mine's Lester," said the beetle. "Want to be a
   real friend?"

"Probably," said Rupert.

"A couple of crummy gophers are chasing me,"
   said Lester. "All you have to do is bellow when
   I tell you to bellow."

"Like this?" said Rupert. He bellowed.

"Even louder," said Lester.

"Here they come now!"

"There he is!" cried the gophers.

"That sneaky, creepy, nasty beetle!"

"Hi, fellas," said Lester. "Meet my old
  friend Rupert."

"*Friend?*" said a gopher. "You don't
  have any friends!"

"Bellow," whispered Lester. "Now!"

Rupert bellowed.

The gophers went flying.

"Nice bellow," said Lester. "So long!"

"Don't you want to play for a while?" asked Rupert.

"With you?" said Lester. "You've got to be kidding."

He hurried away.

An hour later, Lester ran by him again. "Help!" he
said. "A big raccoon is after me. Could you give me
another bellow?"

"I'm pretty busy," said Rupert. "Maybe tomorrow."
And he watched until the raccoon and Lester were
out of sight.

 « 3 »

HERBIE
AND RUPERT
AND DAWN

Herbie and Dawn were taking a nap when
Rupert walked by overhead.
The earth shook.

Herbie and Dawn woke up.

"It's Rupert again," said Herbie.

"Rupert is a pain," said Dawn.

"You woke us up, Rupert," said Dawn.

"You made the earth shake," said Herbie.

"That's what happens when I walk," said Rupert.

"The earth shakes and the trees tremble."

"We know," said Herbie.

"What happens when *you* walk, Herbie?" asked Rupert.

"Not much," said Herbie. "I go

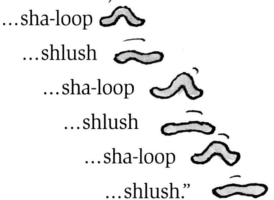

...sha-loop

...shlush

...sha-loop

...shlush

...sha-loop

...shlush."

"I don't even hear that," said Rupert.

"Nobody does," said Herbie.

"That's what's so special," said Dawn.

"When I sit," said Rupert, "I squash
whatever I sit on."

"Big deal," said Dawn.

"When I bellow," said Rupert, "the
whole world hears me."

Rupert bellowed.

"In addition to everything else," said Rupert,

"I am terribly handsome."

"You are?" said Dawn.

"For a rhino, I am," said Rupert.

"Oh," said Dawn.

"We can do *one* thing you can't do, Rupert,"
 said Dawn.
"Oh, yeah?" said Rupert. "What?"
"If we think somebody is a royal pain," said
 Dawn, "we can just *disappear*!"
"How?" asked Rupert.
"Watch!" said Dawn.

Dirt flew...

Then Herbie and Dawn were gone.

"All they did was dig a hole," said Rupert to himself. "I can do that, too." He started to dig.

Rupert dug and dug.

Suddenly his tusk got stuck. Rupert wiggled
this way and that, but he could not get loose.

"What are you doing, Rupert?" asked Herbie.

"I was going to disappear," said Rupert. "Now
   I'm stuck."

"Why didn't you bellow for help?" asked Herbie.

"Nobody would want to help me," said Rupert.

"That's true," said Herbie.

"You know, Rupert," said Dawn, "there's another
thing we can do that you can't do. We can
un-stick stuck rhinos."

"If we want to," said Herbie.

"Do we want to, Herbie?" asked Dawn.

"Sort of," said Herbie. "A little."

"Okay," said Dawn. "Let's dig."
Rupert watched. Pretty soon his tusk was
almost free.

"Look out!" cried Dawn. "I think he's starting
to lean!"

"Run!" cried Herbie.

Rupert crashed.

"Thank you," said Rupert.

"You're welcome," said Dawn.

"Is there anything I can do for *you*?" asked
 Rupert.
"You could practice walking lightly," said Dawn.
"So the earth doesn't shake and the trees don't
 tremble," said Herbie.
"You could learn to bellow softly," said Dawn.
"And sit down very carefully," said Herbie.

"Walk like this?" asked Rupert.

"That's the way," said Herbie.

"Shall I try a bellow?" asked Rupert.

"Go right ahead," said Herbie.

Rupert made a very small sound.

"Was that too loud?" asked Rupert.

"Was what too loud?" asked Herbie.

Herbie and Dawn went to finish their naps.

"I'm sitting down now," called Rupert. "And
I haven't squashed a thing."

"Way to go, Rupert," called Herbie.

"Can we play again soon?" called Dawn.

"As soon as we all wake up," said Rupert.

And they all fell asleep.